A Demon Sandwich

Day S. Grant

Untangling Words Press

Print ISBN: 978-1-966242-06-2

eISBN: 987-1-966242-04-8

Proofreader: Sarah Neeson of 18 Street Editorial

Contents

1. Chapter 1 1
2. Chapter 2 11
3. Chapter 3 15
4. Chapter 4 21
5. Chapter 5 23
6. Chapter 6 31
7. Chapter 7 33
8. Chapter 8 41
9. Chapter 9 45
10. Chapter 10 51
11. Chapter 11 53
12. Chapter 12 59
13. Epilogue 63

About the author 69

Also by Day S. Grant 71

Chapter 1

Madame Abby

THE BELL OVER THE door tinkled with Madame Abby's one o'clock. A blond woman entered and hesitantly wove her way toward the back room. She looked out of place against the sequin red curtains and the mystical wares Madame Abby sold. Her aura was also a slap in the face. But then again, most angel auras almost hurt to be around. This was the first time that Madame Abby was encountering one without forewarning. Angels were nothing but considerate of others.

Given the woman's pencil skirt and polka dot blouse, she likely came straight from the office, which was in and of itself curious. Few angels held typical office jobs, and those who worked rarely left in the middle of the day. Perhaps this woman only worked a half-day on Fridays?

The further the woman's presence diffused through the space, the more off she seemed. The initial shock of her aura had diminished and now hummed in a way that was... well, it wasn't right. At least not right for an angel.

Intrigued, Madame Abby swept past the counter, fanning out her floor-length skirt and letting the bangles around her hips jingle.

"You must be Ms. Skye," she said in greeting.

The woman turned away from the table burning jasmine and amber incense. Her eyes widened in surprise, but with a quick glance around the shop, she seemed to surmise she was the only one arriving at the right time for her appointment. She nodded and said, "You can call me Kylie. Ms. Skye is my mother."

Perhaps her mother was an angel, Madame Abby mused, but that didn't sit right with her. Even half-angels' auras burned a little with their brightness. Kylie's was becoming more and more sweet, like a perfect ambrosia.

"How did you hear about my readings?" Madame Abby asked, leading her client into the back room where there were more red sequin curtains and a small round table with two chairs. Along the wall, her crystal ball and several tarot decks sat on a side table, ready for whatever she needed during an appointment.

"My coworker Rachel recommended you," Kylie murmured as she lowered herself into the chair Madame Abby indicated.

"Rachel Flint? She comes to see me regularly," she said without an ounce of distaste, which was impressive. Rachel was a menace. Abrasive, rude, and just covered in a stabby aura.

"She mentioned you warned her that her boyfriend would leave her for 'some harpy.'" Kylie's wince when she quoted her coworker made it clear to Madame Abby that Rachel wasn't a friend. Which said good things about Kylie's judgment.

Madame Abby barely kept a straight face as she nodded. Rachel had brought her boyfriend Wendel with her for a reading. During previous sessions, Madame Abby had heard lots about Wendel. Rachel had constantly asked her to do readings about him; Madame Abby had evaded answering by giving the excuse that she just couldn't get a good read on him without meeting him first. Which was true, of course. But not the issue. When Rachel finally dragged Wendel in, Madame Abby knew he would be a perfect fit for a siren she knew. Saving the poor man from Rachel wasn't hard; he already had a foot out the door but no reason to leave yet. The reading gave him the push he needed.

"Have you had a reading before?"

"Actually, this is my first."

"And you wanted to do one because of Rachel?" Madame Abby asked cautiously. She eyed the different tarot decks on the side table. Rachel always came for tarot readings, so that's what Kylie would expect. But the normal deck she used for Rachel's trying readings didn't feel right for Kylie.

"Uh, no." Kylie scrunched her face up before admitting, "At happy hour after work last week, where Rachel had been going on and on, my coworkers dared me to come and see if there was a reason for all her fuss. So, here I am." She finished with an apologetic smile.

"So you don't believe in readings?" This was getting odder and odder. How could someone so clearly connected to an angel not believe in the occult?

"It's not that I don't believe in them," Kylie hurried to say. "I just don't know anything about them beyond what Rachel says. To be honest, I've never thought about getting a reading done myself."

"Well, we'll get started and see what comes of it," Madame Abby said.

Her fingers were tingling, and she reached for her special deck. The one with unorthodox cards. That was going to be the right one for Kylie. Normally, she only used the deck for those who weren't human, and sitting with Kylie had made it clear that she was human, even if her aura started with angel and ended in temptation. The power growing in the room told Madame Abby that *something* would come of this.

"Would I be correct that you're adopted?" Madame Abby ventured as she settled into her chair for their session.

"I am!" Kylie's entire face brightened. That explained the aura. If Kylie was adopted by a benevolent angel — and they loved adopting children and creating safe havens — that would tinge her aura. It was clear by her aura's impact that she had been adopted young as well. Probably as an infant in order to be mistaken for an angel on a first meeting. "You really are good. I never talk about it since my mom is just my mom. She doesn't need a qualifier."

Madame Abby nodded in understanding and shuffled her deck. "Do you have a question for me to ask?" she murmured, watching Kylie closely. Her voice was already deepening, which warned her she would enter a trance once she flipped the cards. A trance meant that the reading would be particularly accurate. She loved the accurate ones.

"A question? Was I supposed to have one?"

Kylie was both guileless and sinful. Madame Abby could feel it in the vibrating air of the room. The angel corrupted, yet untouched. Like if the devil turned good.

"No, that's alright," Madame Abby heard herself say. Not having a question wasn't alright, not normally at least. Still, her mind focused in on Kylie's aura, trying to see into the ambrosia through the slap in the face, and her hands flipped over three cards. "Let's see what they say."

The first card was of a werewolf tamed (even among the occult, the myth of the werewolf was popular). Next held two shadows staring out in a blaze of blue. And finally, there was the reaper.

Adrenaline pulsed through Madame Abby. This was too good to be true. A plan formed instantly. She couldn't quite put Kylie directly into the path of the two CEOs who ran Gehenna Industries, but she could get her close. Their logo was wolfsbane, hence the werewolf card, and as demons, their eyes glowed blue like the shadows on the second card. The pair of them lived next door to Madame Abby's friend Markus, a vampire, who was one of the dead and represented by the reaper card. And to top it all off, Markus desperately needed a pet- and house-sitter for the next several months.

Unable to stop the words for the reading in her trance, Madame Abby spilled the beans: "When you first lay eyes on your soulmates' faces, death you will see." She barely managed to mute the 's' on faces, but she was pretty sure Kylie missed it. Not everyone was game to take part in a demon sandwich, regardless of how decadent it could be. She didn't want to scare Kylie off her destiny.

The trance waned, and Madame Abby tore her eyes from the cards to look at Kylie, whose jaw was slack. Maybe she'd scared her anyway.

"I'm going to kill my soulmate if I look in his eyes?" Kylie's gaze flitted around the room, probably deciding if she believed her or not. "I don't want to kill anyone, much less someone perfect for me."

"That is a conundrum," Madame Abby murmured as if she didn't have everything planned out in her head. She pretended to think for a moment before announcing, "I have an idea!"

Kylie's wide eyes pleaded with her.

"Do you love your job?"

"My job? With Rachel?" She made a moue of distaste.

"Put in for an emergency leave of absence so you don't need to go back in. I'll make a call to a friend of mine, Mark, who needs a pet- and house-sitter starting Sunday. You can stay at his place while you figure out how you want to move forward."

"Really? You'd do that?"

"Yes," she declared. This would be perfect. Markus, or Mark as he introduced himself to humans, did desperately need help before he left. "And I'd suggest you don't tell anyone where you're going. You don't want anyone checking up on you and then you seeing their face..." she let her voice trail off as if to imply what could happen.

Kylie violently shook her head no.

Madame Abby grabbed her phone and turned around to hide her smile. Keeping Kylie's location secret until she met the two demons was key. It just wouldn't do to have an adoptive angel parent finding out where she was sending their daughter. Angels normally looked down on the dead, and well, the entire neighborhood where Kylie would be was indeed dead.

Madame Abby stood in the shadows across the street from the coffee shop and smiled. Kylie had absolutely no idea what she was getting herself into. She walked right up to Markus and offered her hand, like shaking the hand of a vampire was something people did every day. Most people, even the magically inclined, were terrified of letting a vampire touch them, especially one with their fangs hanging out and dripping blood. But Kylie didn't look Markus in the face.

She didn't dare to.

Kylie was determined to make sure she didn't hurt anyone. As if she could hurt a soul. Madame Abby scoffed at the mere idea. The girl was so angelic it was, frankly, off-putting. And while she could have been clearer when she'd read Kylie's fortune, where was the fun in that? If Kylie thought looking into her soulmate's face would kill the man, well, that was her problem.

And Madame Abby's fun.

Markus invited Kylie to sit at one of the cute outdoor coffee shop tables, and after just two minutes, he slid his phone across the surface to Kylie. Madame Abby could only imagine it was a photo of Lucy. She wished she could see which one he'd chosen. He was always sending Lucy-photos, never realizing the shock value of each one.

Was Lucy sleeping in the photo? Were her fangs buried in a piece of fruit? Was she hanging upside down or in mid-flight?

With Markus, it was impossible to know what he'd consider appropriate to show someone who wasn't dead that he hoped would pet- and house-sit for him. The photo, however, was apparently benign enough; Kylie only fluttered her eyelashes in shock.

Madame Abby hadn't wanted to spoil the surprise that Kylie would be pet-sitting a bat. A very spoiled bat.

Kylie said something, and Markus looked aghast.

Madame Abby frowned. It was such a shame she couldn't eavesdrop. She loved watching things play out, but she always did it at a distance. Normally, she settled for watching from her crystal ball, but she'd wanted some fresh air today. And since Kylie had just fallen into her lap, she thought she'd witness the action in person. Rarely did she matchmake new clients. Typically, she had to get to know them a little better. But Fate was kind sometimes.

After a few more exchanges, Markus picked his phone up off the table. Madame Abby was almost positive that his lips formed the name Gehenna Industries. This was better than she could have hoped. She'd expected to have to wait at least a few days, if not a handful of weeks, before Kylie finally met Markus's neighbors. Radic and Tinral, according to their reputations and what Markus had told her over the years, didn't meddle or pry into others' affairs. They were unlikely to investigate Markus's pet- and house-sitter. They'd probably just assume that his house-sitter was like him: dead and partial to blood.

But if Markus was messaging the pair right then, they must need someone to fill a vacancy in their company. Madame Abby already knew nothing had been posted online — she'd checked — but Markus could have heard it straight from the horse's mouth. If that was the case, Kylie would be in Radic and Tinral's hands before Madame Abby could arrange a watch-party with the others.

There wasn't a moment to lose. She needed to head back and start making calls, schedule the bouncers to keep the uninitiated out, and so much more. Madame Abby set off down the street back toward her shop. Everyone was going to be envious of the match she'd orchestrated. They'd all want to watch and celebrate her success. She hoped Radic and Tinral held off till the weekend... it'd be awful to miss the good stuff.

Chapter 2

Radic & Tinral

What time is the secretary supposed to arrive? Radic asked, stalking back and forth between their desks while staring down at the slowly filling employee parking lot.

At 9 a.m. like everyone else, Tinral answered without looking up. He sat at his desk, reviewing the paperwork for their latest acquisition — a windmill farm just outside of town. Their company's mission was to make sure that there was no hell on earth by preserving and restoring natural resources and protecting wildlife.

Ten minutes. That seemed like forever. They were going to need to change her start time Radic decided. It was inconvenient to have their secretary start after them. Tinral silently reminded Radic that it was her first day, so they'd have to go easy on her. As it was, it was a miracle that their neighbor Markus had called and said he'd found someone who could fill in for at least the next three months. Their former secretary, Hundfer, a gargoyle who was stone at night rather than during the day, had quit on Friday after his psychic had told him he needed to move on.

Normally, they wouldn't have even considered hiring one of the living as their secretary, but Markus had a knack for finding what people needed — there was a reason he was a well-known private investigator that even non-vampires went to. Had it been anyone else's recommendation, they would have at least put the candidate through a rigorous interview, but they'd hired Kylie Skye while still on the phone with Markus. Kylie had emailed them her resume Saturday night, and everything had fallen into place. It seemed perfect. She had five years of experience as a secretary at a respectable firm and managed the schedules for several lower-level managers at once. Handling Radic and Tinral's two schedules wouldn't be too challenging for her, particularly since they were never more than a room apart from each other.

"You know," Tinral finally said aloud, annoyed with Radic's pacing, "if you're that impatient to be reminded about our schedule, you could just pull it up on your computer. It's going to take her a little while to get situated and decipher how Hundfer organized things, even with the detailed instructions he left her."

"I feel like something is crawling under my skin," Radic groused. "We're missing something."

Tinral narrowed his eyes at his partner and reflected on how he himself was feeling. He wasn't amped up in the least. In fact, he was calm. Perhaps calmer than normal.

"You're right. We're missing something. You're agitated, and I'm subdued." Tinral stood up and stared at the parking lot, cutting off Radic's path. Radic spun around and adjusted his circuit to the smaller space. Unease filled them both as they watched their employees arrive, but neither of them could put a finger on the cause.

As the clock chimed nine, a knock on their door echoed through the office.

She's punctual, Radic scoffed, not relieved by their new employee's arrival like he had thought he'd be.

"Come in," Tinral called.

The second the door cracked open, Tinral and Radic found it hard to breathe. By the time their new secretary had finished pushing the door open, they didn't know if they should stay away from her or strip her naked. Both options were equally compelling.

Her blond hair fell over her shoulder, and sinful lashes lined her downcast eyes. Radic wanted to tip her chin up. Tinral wanted to brush his thumb along her cheekbones. The pencil skirt she wore hugged her curves so tightly they wouldn't be able to cut it off her, but the fantasy still held merit. Everything about her was light and airy in their dark, paneled office. Her presence screamed angel, but the rest of her was pure temptation. If they could just stroke her until she was a shuddering mess, things would be alright in the world.

"Mr. Tin, Mr. Rad?" she said uncertainly, not raising her eyes fully to look at them. "Is everything alright?"

It irritated Radic that Markus had given her their sanitized names. Their more human-like names. He wanted to hear her saying his real name. Maybe crying it out in ecstasy. Yeah, that sounded more like it.

"Of course," Tinral murmured. *There'll be time for that,* he assured Radic, equally enthralled with their new secretary. "Ms. Skye, right?"

Her laugh hit them both below the belt, and their knees threatened to give out.

"Just Kylie is fine."

We need her to raise her eyes, Radic groaned out.

"Kylie," Tinral continued evenly, as if his cock wasn't trying to break free from his slacks as he fought the urge to bend her over his or Radic's desk. "Why don't we all have a seat? We can go over your duties."

I have some things she could help out with, Radic bit out.

And if she's angelic as she seems? Are you really willing to burn?

If she was an angel, she'd have shown some sort of reaction to us. It's not like we're hard to miss.

Which was true enough. One look at their eyes, their glowing blue eyes, and no one had any doubts that Radic and Tinral were demons. But she hadn't looked them in the face. She hadn't seen that they had no iris or pupils, just a solid glow.

Thankfully, Kylie moved to the chair in front of Tinral's desk. It was the one he'd gestured to, and that worked in his favor. He sat down in his seat across from her, thankful his hard-on was hidden. Radic sat down in the second seat across from Tinral, beside Kylie. His arousal wasn't as well hidden, but it'd have to do for now. At least until they figured out what Kylie was. Markus hadn't sent them a word of warning. He said she was one of the living, which might be possible, but they couldn't be sure yet. They really hoped Markus was right though...

Chapter 3

Kylie

KYLIE HELD HERSELF STILL as her two bosses lowered themselves into their seats. The closer they came, the stronger the smoky myrrh scent became. She couldn't tell if the smell came from one of them or both. But it made her think of decadence. Much like their office did with its dark colors and plush carpets. Given how her heels sunk into the carpet, it'd probably be the perfect cushion for her knees...

Seconds ticked by, and their eyes bored into her. Her heart raced along with her inappropriate fantasy. Everything in her pushed her to glance up and see exactly what they looked like. But she couldn't risk satisfying her curiosity. What if she killed them?

No. She had to keep her eyes down.

Mark hadn't been put off that she wouldn't look him in the face when she'd met him at the coffee shop two days ago. Hopefully, Mr. Tin and Mr. Rad would just think she was demure. Demure wasn't her natural state, but maybe she'd learn. She had at least three months that she'd be bat-sitting at Mark's house to get it down pat. It still boggled her mind that Mark had a pet bat, but to each his own. She wasn't going to judge him when she needed what he was offering her — a place to stay where she wouldn't be bothered by friends who she might kill with a single look.

But not looking at her bosses was much harder than she would have thought. Half of her wished Mark hadn't been so solicitous about finding her a way to occupy her days while she stayed at his place. The other half... well, the other half was salivating over her bosses without even seeing their faces.

One of them, she wasn't sure which yet, was wearing a gray suit. He had broad shoulders and a trim waist that would look great pumping between her legs. The other was in a blue suit. His shoulders were just as broad, but his frame was stout and perfect for climbing astride. Neither looked like they had an ounce of fat on their bodies. At least from what she could see with their suits on. And she could see *much* more than she expected when it came down to their pants.

Kylie had no idea what was happening to her. Normally, she got to know a man before she really gave much thought to what he looked like in the nude. And here she was, her first day on the job, doing more than mentally undressing both her bosses. Both of whom seemed impressively endowed if the way their zippers molded to their assets was to be believed. What was wrong with her?

When neither man spoke, Kylie ventured, "Mark didn't tell me much about the position." She definitely wanted them in all the positions.

"What *did* he tell you?" the man to her left in the blue suit snapped. His voice dragged delightfully across her senses, making her imagine what she could drive him to do in order to work out that anger. She wasn't surprised that he didn't like her at first blush. No one did. She was apparently an acquired taste. And even after people got used to her, she still never felt like she fit in.

"Mr. Rad," the man across the desk said in a strained voice. It sounded vaguely like a warning. Kylie wished she could look at their expressions to decipher what was going on. At least she knew that the man in blue was Mr. Rad and the man in gray was Mr. Tin. That was more than she knew when she'd sat down.

"When Mark heard I didn't have plans for my days while I'm pet-sitting, he said he knew just the thing for me to do and asked if I would mind helping you two out since your secretary left," she said quickly to placate them both. She didn't want to rub them the wrong way before she'd even had a chance to get things in hand. And she really wanted to get both of them *in hand*.

The room fell oddly still as she finished speaking. Her head started to rise of its own accord, but she caught herself before her eyes followed its lead.

"You're taking care of Lucy?" Mr. Tin asked. His voice was barely above a whisper.

"Well, yes. I know she isn't the typical pet, but..." She shrugged.

"And staying in... Mark's house?" Mr. Rad continued.

"Yes?" Kylie suddenly felt unsure of herself. Something about how Mr. Rad had said Mark's name sounded wrong. Like he'd never said it before, which was odd. He had called them while sitting at the coffee shop with her. They were clearly well acquainted. They knew Mark's pet bat and likely that he insisted she'd get lonely if left alone for more than a night or two, which led to house-sitters rather than just pet-sitters.

Silence stretched, and she fought the urge to look at their faces instead of the sleek top of Mr. Tin's desk — a desk that she was certain would show her flushed reflection if she leaned over it. Both men sat still as stone. Unable to take it any longer, she prompted, "About my duties?"

"Of course," Mr. Tin said from across the desk. His voice sounded like gravel — the good kind of gravel — and Kylie squeezed her legs together as she imagined that rumble traveling through her body. "It's wonderful you could start on such short notice. Hundfer, your predecessor, hadn't wanted to leave so suddenly, but it couldn't be helped."

Hundfer? Now that was a name. Kylie didn't know what to make of it.

Mr. Tin continued, "He wrote out a detailed description of his organization process, which should be helpful. Though his process was unique, so it might take a bit to get familiarized with and adapt it to your own methods."

"For today, you need to handle people who arrive for meetings, call in, and possibly shift things around if something comes up," Mr. Rad ground out from beside her. As far as she could tell, he hadn't moved an inch. She wondered how long he'd resent her presence. It generally took several weeks for people to come around. And would he stay so grouchy if she took care of anything that *came up*?

"That shouldn't be a problem," she said, striving to remain professional despite her horny thoughts. "I assume the desk outside your office is where I'll be working?"

"Yes," Mr. Tin murmured. Her body automatically tilted forward like he had his own gravitational pull.

"You should go there now. We have work to do," Mr. Rad snapped, causing her to jerk back an inch.

"Of course," she squeaked and hurried away from the two very hot men she'd be working for over the next three months. Why did she find even the surly one attractive?

Shutting their office door behind her, Kylie took a deep breath and sagged against it. The pair of them were a lot to take in. She both wanted to be in their presence and escape from the sexual compulsion that pounded at her when she was near them. They both dredged up the dirtiest office fantasies her mind could come up with. Bent over their desks? Yes please! Laid out beside their computer to be devoured? She wouldn't turn that down. Both of them together? Mind-blowing. How was she going to face them again?

As the complete silence around her penetrated her fantasizing, she realized she didn't hear a single sound coming from inside the office. She glanced at the door. It seemed odd that they'd have a fully soundproof door.

But it wasn't soundproof.

She knew she'd been able to hear them call her in without any problem. Maybe they just weren't big talkers and focused on their own tasks. That had to be it.

With that thought, she headed to her desk—her large, dark gray desk — to see to her own work. She needed to get up-to-speed with whatever Hundfer had left for her, and the phone could start ringing any minute. She didn't even know when the first meeting of the day was.

Rounding the desk, she saw a notebook with a sticky note that read, "For the new secretary." She tried to sit down in the ergonomic desk chair but had to spend at least ten minutes adjusting it to a usable setup. Whoever her predecessor was, he had apparently liked his seat back curved so that it only touched his spine and not his shoulders. Still not particularly comfortable in the chair, she flipped open the notebook.

The first page was titled, "Most Important Things to Remember." Smiling, Kylie looked at the first bullet point. And immediately frowned.

"It goes without saying, but Radic and Tinral should never be scheduled separately. If you absolutely must do so, it can't be more than a room apart. It's tempting to forget. DON'T."

Shaking her head, she glanced at her bosses' office door. That was just plain weird. It had been odd enough that the two CEOs shared an office, but they were always together, too? And why would that go without saying? And were those nicknames Hundfer had for Mr. Tin and Mr. Rad? This was just plain weird.

Chapter 4

Madame Abby

Madame Abby slipped into her back room and waved her hand over her crystal ball, not bothering to take it off the side table. She already had it keyed up, and her favorite future threesome appeared in its depths. Grinning, she zoomed in to see what they were up to.

She knew it was Kylie's third day working right under Radic and Tinral. She'd missed their initial meeting, but the bits she'd seen so far had been promising. The tension was off the charts, but from what she could tell, Kylie still refused to look her bosses in the face, which was likely driving them insane.

And was probably why Radic, in his typical blue suit, was standing behind what looked like a new chair for Kylie's desk and gesturing to her to sit down. Tinral was kneeling to the side of the chair, clearly insisting that he adjust it for her. Kylie looked both mortified by their attention and a little like she was going to hyperventilate from panting. While Madame Abby could see their lips moving, she couldn't hear what they were saying, which was always a shame.

Normally, demon soulmates sensed each other immediately and joined as soon as they could. Madame Abby guessed that Kylie's aura was throwing them off. If they mistook her for an angel, they'd never touch her regardless of the pull. Death by angel was especially painful for a demon, from what Madame Abby had heard. So they were being cautious.

Madame Abby had read her cards several times, and what she'd seen in her crystal ball supported her findings. The two demons were leaving Kylie alone, but by Friday, they'd reach their limit. She just hoped they could wait until the evening. Otherwise, her watch-party would be a bust.

With a wave of her hand, she wiped the scene away and then hustled back out to the front. No one had come in while she was in back, but she'd known they wouldn't. She only slipped back and checked when she knew there'd be a lull. As she walked back to the counter, she straightened a summoning stone and pulled the love potions to the edge of their shelf. She was running low and would need to get some more from one of the witches who preferred selling through her shop rather than setting up their own.

Back at the counter, she checked her guest list. Already half her guests had RSVP'd that they wouldn't miss a dual-demon-soul-mate watch-party. The other half would likely respond by the end of tomorrow, which would give her just enough time on Friday to scrounge up party hors d'oeuvres.

Chapter 5

Radic & Tinral

Radic and Tinral stood at their one-way window with the best view of Markus's dark red house. And waited. They'd come straight home after their last meeting of the day without swinging back through the office in order to get home before Kylie.

The past week had been excruciating. They'd constantly found reasons to call her into their office or go out by her desk just to be near her. She probably thought they were the most forgetful individuals ever. But they just couldn't stay away from her. The initial shock of her had faded, and all they felt was uncontrollable desire, the likes of which they'd never experienced before. It was disconcerting and impossible to suppress.

Despite all indications that Kylie was indeed human, Radic had been compelled to confirm. Tinral hadn't liked it, but he could see that, between the two of them, Radic was closer to losing control; if he dragged her into their office and took her on the desk or against the windows like they were both thinking of, they'd terrify her. Tinral had relented and let Radic arrange a small incident yesterday, on Kylie's fourth day of work. They'd asked Ophelia, a vampire in the office, to drop off some papers with Kylie, but accidentally nick her with one of her sharpened fingernails.

Since Kylie had put half the staff on edge with her initial angelic effect (though thankfully none of their employees were bothering her with the same persistence as Radic and Tinral were or they'd have had to fire them on the spot), Ophelia had just shrugged and did as they asked. A few drops of red blood, not gold, fell on Kylie's desk, confirming what Tinral already knew. Kylie was human.

Radic and Tinral had swooped in with a band-aid and hovered solicitously, watching the way Kylie's breath sped up in their presence and the way her legs clenched together as if there were a throbbing between them that needed relief. Relief that they were both a hair's breadth from offering to give her there on the spot. The news that she was definitely a living, breathing human made it through the office in the next half hour and the pervasive tension since her arrival diminished significantly.

Much to Radic's dismay, he became more aggravated rather than less at the news. Tinral had pointed out that might be a potential outcome, but an I-told-you-so was never necessary between the two of them. Still, that led them to standing in their house, staring at Markus's place and waiting. Waiting to witness the show that their neighbor across the way said happened every evening before they got home. It should start in approximately — Tinral checked his watch — two minutes.

Right on time, Kylie pulled her sky-blue car into Markus's driveway. No one had missed her car in the neighborhood. Every vehicle owned by the inhabitants was a dark color. Every single one. The dead didn't do light, airy colors. Kylie slid out of her car in her skintight pencil skirt that Radic and Tinral saw whenever they closed their eyes, and a loose cream blouse that teased them endlessly. She wore the same thing to work every day; only the colors varied.

They hadn't told her they lived next door. The temptation to go over would have been too great. But now that they knew for sure that she wouldn't burn them to a crisp on contact, they needed to make a move. While Tinral had been calmer, if hornier than ever the past week, Radic was not okay. And he would remain so until they got Kylie to look them in the eye. They needed to see her. All of her.

We need to wait, Tinral reminded Radic. *Let her do her thing and then go over. Let her settle.*

Radic crossed his arms in response, his body a rigid line of tension.

Five minutes after heading inside, Kylie strutted back out the front door. She'd changed into leggings and a light pink sweater, which was more or less what their neighbor said she wore in the evenings. Hanging from her left hand was Markus's pet bat, Lucy. Given how Kylie had yet to look at the face of a single person in the office, Radic and Tinral were fairly certain she had no clue Markus was a vampire. If she hadn't seen his fangs, she could have missed it. They both wondered how he'd explained Lucy to her.

We should change before we go over, Tinral muttered. They were still in their suits. Radic grunted at the suggestion. He disliked jeans with an unmatchable passion that Tinral didn't share. *It might put her more at ease since she's no longer in office clothes,* Tinral reasoned.

Without a word, Radic turned away from the window once Kylie and Lucy rounded the corner and walked out of sight. They had plenty of time to change without worrying about Kylie's return to the house. Lucy's nightly walk was always at least thirty minutes and, if Markus was to be believed, essential to her health.

They walked through their living room, not needing to turn on the lights to see, weaving between the dark-toned furniture on their way toward the back of the house and their bedroom. Splitting apart when they reached their double queen — a bed that was equivalent to a queen and a half wide — they headed to their respective closets on each side of the room.

Ten minutes later, they were back at the window, waiting for Kylie's return, wearing dark wash jeans and holding cups of steaming black coffee. Radic wore a blue tee, as usual, and Tinral a gray. Twenty-two minutes after that, Kylie and Lucy returned from their walk.

Let's go, Radic snapped.

We need to wait at least five more minutes. You remember that time we went over to Markus's after Lucy's walk and had to watch him hand-feed Lucy?

That gave Radic pause. Lucy was a messy bat. She splattered fruit bits everywhere when in a feeding frenzy. Then she crawled around and licked up every last bit. Tinral and Radic hadn't enjoyed being licked by her....

Fine. Five minutes.

After enough time had passed for Kylie to feed Lucy, they walked, or in Radic's case stalked, next door. Together, they knocked, and a minute later, Kylie opened the door. Tinral felt his knees go a little weak while his dick grew stiffer. Radic gripped the doorjamb to stop himself from reaching for her.

"I'm sorry, but Mark is visiting family out of the country," Kylie explained, not lifting her gaze above their chests.

"We're here to see you," Tinral said.

"Really?" Her face scrunched up in confusion.

She doesn't even know it's us, and she opened the door, Radic snapped in irritation, before saying, "Let us in, Kylie."

"Mr. Rad? Mr. Tin?" She hastily let them in. "What are you doing here? Did something go wrong at the office?"

"Everything's fine, Kylie," Tinral soothed, taking in how out-of-place Kylie's light pink sweater and blond hair were in Markus's black and burgundy home.

Okay, I'm a little happy you made sure she wasn't an angel, he said to Radic, but Radic was already moving in on Kylie.

"Mr. Rad?" she squeaked when her hip bumped against the entry table, and she was trapped. Her sugary scent assailed them both. It was just as decadent here as in the office.

Easy, Radic, Tinral counseled.

Radic reached out and slid his hand under Kylie's chin, causing a whimper to slip past her lips that gutted them both. Unable to stop himself, Tinral stroked his knuckles along her cheek.

"Why won't you look at us?" Tinral coaxed, since Radic was in no mood to tread lightly.

"Well, it's, um," she stammered, blushing.

"You can tell us."

She better tell us, Radic said.

"Well, you see, um, on a dare, I went to a tarot reader a week and a half ago," she said.

"Which one?" Tinral asked in surprise. That would have been just days before she moved into Markus's house and started working as their secretary.

"Madame Abby."

"On X Street?"

"Yes."

She's good, Radic said with a touch of hesitancy. Madame Abby was a fate of some renown, especially given her young age. Her readings tended to be accurate. Not always in the way her client expected. But accurate, nonetheless.

"And what did she read in the cards?" Tinral prompted Kylie over the scrambling noises of Lucy in her enclosure down the hall. Radic was still holding her chin, urging her face up. Her eyes fluttered shut, and she let him lift her face. But her eyes stayed resolutely shut.

"That when I first laid eyes on my soulmate's face, he would be dead," she whispered.

Radic and Tinral exchanged a look. Their entire neighborhood was dead. Their clients were dead. She was surrounded by the dead.

"So you reached out to Mark," Tinral reasoned, forcing out the simplified name. That made sense. Move to where everyone was dead. Where she'd likely find her soulmate. But then why wouldn't she look at them?

Unless she thinks she'll kill her soulmate rather than that he'd be one of the dead, Radic pointed out.

"No, I didn't know Mark. Madame Abby assured me that all would be okay, and she had a friend who needed a pet-sitter. Next thing I know, I'd moved in here and started working for you."

"She sent you here?" Radic asked. His voice was rough with shock, but no longer angry. *This can't be a coincidence.*

Absolutely not, Tinral agreed. They were too drawn to her for it to be a coincidence.

Kylie nodded against Radic's hand.

"What were Madame Abby's exact words?" Tinral prompted Kylie. They needed the exact words. The difference in a single syllable could change everything.

"After she flipped over the cards, she said, 'When you first lay eyes on your soulmate's face, death you will see.'"

This is it, Radic whispered. His thumb slid along Kylie's jawline.

But we have to ease into it, Tinral said, his fingers sliding into her hair. The silky strands were a caress he didn't know he'd been missing. He couldn't stop himself from plunging deeper and fisting her hair. This was why he'd been so at peace. This was why Radic had been so wound up.

Their minds spun. It was all a matter of punctuation and s's. Kylie was terrified that she would kill her soulmate by looking at his face, but in truth, her soulmates were already dead. Madame Abby sent her straight to them.

Chapter 6

Madame Abby

A HUSHED "OOOH" TRICKLED through Madame Abby's guests. Eight had already arrived and just in the nick of time, too. That afternoon, she'd set up a large white projection screen in her main shop to enhance the image clarity of her crystal ball for the watch-party's enjoyment. She'd also slid her display tables to the side and lit musk and strawberry-rose incense to set the mood.

Everyone present was sure that Kylie had just outed Madame Abby as the reason she was standing before the two demons, Radic and Tinral. Lipreading wasn't always perfect, but when it was her own name, Madame Abby was pretty good at recognizing it.

"You so rarely get credit with matchmaking," Beatrice, a fellow mystic, muttered to Lucinda and Royal, a pair of vampires who often attended Madame Abby's watch-parties.

"This is the first time I've seen her mentioned by her matches," Lucinda concurred, squeezing Royal's thigh where her hand rested.

She'd been with Royal for the last fifty years, ever since she'd turned him. Madame Abby had had nothing to do with their whirlwind romance — as she hadn't been alive at the time — but the three had become good friends.

"Look at their faces," Ervin, an orange monster, chortled, pointing at Tinral and Radic. The two's rapt expressions were worshipful as they stared at Kylie, who still refused to look at them. There was significantly more awe involved than the lust fueled gazes Madame Abby had seen them giving her all week.

"They totally know!" Purlin shrieked. Her siren voice drew every eye in the shop. There was a certain pitch that mermaids could hit that made it impossible to ignore them.

The guests immediately broke into speculation. Madame Abby silently agreed with Purlin. Tinral and Radic knew Kylie was their soulmate. The real question was, would they tell her and then set about seducing her or do just the opposite?

The bell over the front door sounded, and the warlock and hybrid bouncers she'd hired for the evening let another guest through. Burty, a tree nymph, dashed in with a fluttering of her delicate wings and went straight to Madame Abby.

"What did I miss?" she asked, whipping off her jacket and drawing Ervin's eyes. With a smile, Madame Abby quickly filled her in before shooing her on to join the others.

Already, the night was a great success. And it was just beginning.

Chapter 7

Kylie

Kylie was finding it hard to breathe with her bosses so close and their hands on her. Mr. Rad continued to tilt her head up toward their faces, and she could feel Mr. Tin's fist grip her hair. There was no way she could open her eyes without looking them in the face, but she also couldn't bring herself to protest when she'd wanted their hands on her all week long. So, she kept her eyes shut and just breathed in her bosses' arousing scent, fighting the urge to tremble under their attention. She couldn't believe she hadn't melted into a puddle already.

"Have you eaten?" Mr. Tin asked from above her.

She went to shake her head, but with them holding her, she couldn't. Instead, her tongue darted out nervously over her lips, and she whispered, "No," a little more breathily than she would have liked. But with all the implications of eating that her mind supplied, it was impossible to keep her voice level.

Mr. Rad's hand shifted on her chin, and the rough pad of his thumb ran over her lip, dragging it down. Kylie lost her battle with her body and trembled. What she wouldn't do to have him push his thumb into her mouth for her tongue to play with.

Both men had been highly solicitous all week, even if Mr. Rad's attentions had been accompanied by irritation. After the first day, it occurred to her she hadn't caused his mood. If she had, he could have easily avoided her the rest of the week. Instead, she'd found Mr. Rad and Mr. Tin ready to assist her in every way as she figured out her predecessor's complicated system for running their lives. They had practically hovered around her, swamping her with near-constant desire for things she really shouldn't have been thinking about while at work. She imagined that their attentions meant that they liked her and didn't find her off-putting like most people did. And given their immediate proximity, she knew she hadn't been completely off target.

"We'll make some dinner then," Mr. Tin said inches from her ear. She had no idea when he'd leaned toward her, and she couldn't open her eyes to see if he was still there. On the back of her eyelids, flashes of all they could do with her on a dinner table assailed her.

After a moment, Mr. Rad's fingers released her and slid along her cheek as Mr. Tin's tightened in her hair once more before slipping away. The loss of contact was a devastating shock to her system.

"I'll see what we have to work with in the fridge," Mr. Rad said from her left, sounding like he'd turned away. Down the hallway, Kylie could hear Lucy fluttering around in her aviary that took up half the kitchen. She seemed excited that they had guests.

"Come, we'll get you settled in at the counter," Mr. Tin murmured, taking her hand and hooking it over his forearm by the crook of his elbow.

Kylie didn't want to be hanging off her boss's arm because it had to be an HR violation, but she also didn't think she could follow the two men into the kitchen without her legs giving out. When Mr. Tin flexed his arm minutely to support her, it was all she could do not to hyperventilate. He could easily lift her and move her wherever he wanted her to be, which she desperately wanted him to do. Part of her wished she feared the two of them, because that seemed like a logical reaction to be having. But that was decidedly not why her knees were failing her and her lungs were seizing. Not at all.

Unable to do anything else with her eyes closed, Kylie let him turn her away from the door and lead her down the hall toward the kitchen in back. Feeling it was safe enough as they started moving, she opened her eyes a crack and watched the black marble floor as they walked. Beside her, Mr. Tin was wearing jeans. She had noticed both men at the door were wearing jeans when she'd opened it, but it was just hitting her that her bosses weren't wearing their suits. They'd changed after work before coming and checking on her. She was pretty sure she'd always left the office before them, but they had had a meeting out of the office. Maybe it ended early.

Distracted by the exposed forearm under her fingertips, Kylie surreptitiously shifted her fingers to trace a vein in Mr. Tin's arm. When he spoke, she almost jumped out of her skin.

"Besides Lucy's fruit," Mr. Tin said, "what can we expect to find in the fridge?"

"Not much," she answered honestly. "I went to the grocery store on Sunday when I moved in, so it's pretty barren now."

"Markus didn't leave anything in there?" he asked. He sounded perturbed by the idea, which made no sense.

"No. He said that since I'd be here for three months, I should have the whole thing to myself." Noting the name change, Kylie followed up with, "Does he prefer to be called Markus? Madame Abby told me his name was Mark, and he didn't correct me when we met to discuss what Lucy needed."

Kylie could have sworn that Mr. Tin tensed at her question. She gave his arm a little appreciative squeeze in response before she could stop herself. It was as hard as steel.

"Mark is what he uses when he's trying to be extra... presentable," he explained after a moment.

Taking a chance since they'd reached the counter, Kylie let her eyes sweep up and saw that Mr. Rad was standing before the open fridge. His tee-shirt was blue, much like his suits. She almost laughed, but the view was a little too encompassing. It was a tight shirt. His suits, apparently, hid a lot of muscle. Much like Mr. Tin, whose arm she was still clutching. She should probably let go, but she couldn't quite make herself do so.

"You can call us Radic and Tinral, by the way," Mr. Rad said without turning around. His voice changed from his normal aggressive to just gruff.

There were those names again. The ones from Hundfer's instructions. "O-okay," Kylie said, wondering if the nicknames were an *out-of-the-office* policy.

Lucy chose that moment to make the squeaky chirps that Kylie had been told meant she wanted people to look at her and admire her. Since she felt Mr. Tin — no, Tinral — turn toward Lucy minutely, Kylie kept drinking in Mr. Rad's — or Radic's — back.

"How does strawberry-balsamic chicken thighs over potatoes and vegetables sound?" Radic asked as he turned around. Kylie immediately dropped her eyes as he moved. Though she barely knew her bosses, she liked them too much to risk killing either with a glance.

Fighting her frustration at living like a freaking Medusa, she said, "Fancy? And like I don't have any of the ingredients."

"We'll all go back to our place," Tinral said. His arm pulled her around back toward the front door. Stumbling, she clung to him.

"Your place?" she asked, confused. They were taking her to their place? They lived together? That particular fact was enough to pull her from her lust-induced haze. Kylie imagined most men didn't want to be joined at the hip 24/7—both at work and at home. That seemed like a lot of time together.

"Did you already feed Lucy?" Radic asked, walking over to Lucy's aviary. Lucy darted around her aviary and chirped several more times, greeting Radic and showing off her wings. At least that's how Mark, or Markus, explained her actions. Kylie had her doubts.

"Yeah. Right after her walk. Markus was very particular about that."

"Particular is one way to put it," Mr. R— no, Radic muttered. Kylie suppressed a giggle at the comment. Apparently, Radic found Lucy a little disconcerting.

Tinral started walking them toward the front door, and Radic immediately fell into step behind them. Their presence surrounded her, making her feel shaky all over again.

"I'm sure I have enough food to manage dinner for myself. I wouldn't want to impose—"

"Nonsense," Radic scoffed behind her. Kylie could swear he muttered something like, "As if you could ever be an imposition."

They were at the door before she knew it. Tinral let her pull away and grab her phone, but when she reached for her car keys, he told her she wouldn't need them.

"We live next door," he murmured.

Not only did they know where Markus lived since he was their friend, but they'd known she was just next door all week and had said nothing. She rolled her eyes. Why would they say anything? It's not like they owed her an accounting of everywhere they were when not at work.

"Oh," was all she could think to say in response as she blinked several times at their jeans and the generous bulges they each sported. If only they'd put their packages to good use and work her over.

Trying to keep it together, Kylie walked out of Markus's house and locked the door with the keypad and fingerprint scanner. Radic took possession of her hand and hooked it over his arm while Tinral placed his hand at the small of her back. With her sandwiched between them, they made their way down the walkway and to the sidewalk.

Since Radic and Tinral were firmly at her sides, Kylie lifted her eyes and looked at their home with a new interest. Like Markus's place, and honestly, every other place in the neighborhood, the house looked somber. It was painted a slate gray-blue and had black accents. They swept inside where the lights were dimmed, but not out. There was a clean, cool smell to their place that contrasted with a cinnamon scent she'd noticed in Markus's house. To her surprise, even their furniture was dark. Very nice, but dark. It made the red accents in Markus's place look aggressively bright.

"Did I miss a memo about the neighborhood?" she forced herself to ask. She felt a little out of place in her light pink sweater. At least in Markus's place, she was just a dilution of the red.

"What do you mean?" Tinral asked.

"I noticed the houses are... well, they seem to be painted darker colors than I'm used to seeing. And while your house is only the second I've been in, it's decorated a bit more on the noir side of things. It's nice, of course. Lovely," Kylie added quickly. She didn't want to offend them. "It's just darker than I've seen in most people's homes."

Radic cleared his throat. "We prefer darker colors."

"But we love the light colors you wear," Tinral said practically over Radic's comment.

"Of course," Radic said. He sounded appalled that she might have taken his comment to be about how she dressed, which had never crossed her mind.

"Alright," she chuckled, shaking her head. Like they could offend her. They'd be offended if they knew exactly how dirty her thoughts had been about them, both while at work and next door in bed.

The pair took her to the kitchen, which was to the left of the front room they'd entered. In comparison to Lucy's near constant background noise in the evening, their house was silent. Together, they deposited her at the counter and swept around to the far side. Kylie quickly dropped her inquisitive gaze away from the near-black stainless-steel appliances and to the sparkling black granite countertop.

"Wine?" Tinral suggested.

"I'd love some. I've been meaning to message Markus and ask if he'd mind if I enjoyed a bottle from his wine cellar."

"I'd recommend against it," Radic said immediately.

"Oh, is he particularly protective of his collection?"

"Something like that," Tinral said as he uncorked a bottle of white wine, quickly pouring her a glass. When he passed it to her, it seemed like he intentionally lingered, making their fingers brush. At least, that's how it felt. Privately, Kylie hoped that was the case.

Tinral poured two more glasses and came around the counter to sit with her as Radic got to work.

"Radic's the better cook. I'm the better eater," Tinral said by way of explanation.

"When I cook, I just get less hungry," Radic said with a shrug of his broad shoulders, which pulled his blue tee tighter across his chest. Kylie barely managed to swallow her sip of wine between imagining Tinral eating her and appreciating the muscled view Radic provided.

Chapter 8

Madame Abby

"Come on!" Ervin yelled at the projection. "Just look him in the eye!"

Madame Abby could sympathize with the big orange guy. Watching a silent conversation was not overly enthralling. Radic was cooking, and Kylie and Tinral were just drinking wine. They'd likely have to wait through an entire meal for anything to happen. Which was good for the guests who hadn't arrived yet.

"Madame Abby, does she just need to look one of them in the eye for their connection to click into place?" Burty asked.

"I'm not sure," Madame Abby admitted. "It could be she has to look each of them in the eye or look at them both at the same time. We'll have to wait and see." Demon pairs like Radic and Tinral weren't the most common occurrence. She'd paired someone with a demon before, but not with a duo.

"At least with the two of them catching on to what is happening," Purlin said while wiping a wet cloth over herself since she'd been away from water for too long, "we know it'll happen tonight."

"But isn't it weird for them when things move into the bedroom?" Royal asked from beside his vampire love. "I wouldn't want to have a threesome of any kind with one of my siblings present, much less participating."

"No, honey, it's not like that," Lucinda said with a laugh.

"It's a common misconception," Madame Abby concurred. "Demon pairs aren't siblings. They're always from different families. They're soul-bound best-friends. From my knowledge, a demon pair needs to meet by the age of ten, and then when puberty hits, that's when the binding takes place. At that point, they can never be separated from each other; it's physically impossible."

There were hums of agreement from several guests. Demons kept parts of their lore and traditions close to the vest, like others did. And it was beyond rude to ask. There were certain things about monsters that Madame Abby could only speculate about, and she would never ask Ervin or any other monster she knew. Same for sirens like Purlin and nymphs like Burty. Vampires were mostly an open book as far as Madame Abby knew, though she and Beatrice had something in the works for Markus and a vampire Beatrice did readings for. She'd never witnessed a vampire-vampire pairing, but she expected it to be much the same as other vampire joinings she'd seen.

"Since we have some time," she waved her hand at the uneventful projection, "let's eat."

Her guests rose and headed over to her refreshments, and Madame Abby headed to the door to see if the bouncers needed anything. They'd both worked her little parties before, so at least this time she didn't have to break it to one of them what they were in for as the night wore on.

Chapter 9

Radic &Tinral

She hasn't had too much to drink, has she? Tinral asked, trying not to hover over Kylie and Radic on the couch by finishing the dishes from dinner.

Radic gazed down at Kylie's shoulder, where her sweater had slipped off. He resisted tracing its edge with his lips, but he didn't think he could wait much longer. That was asking too much of him. *No, but we shouldn't refill her glass. We don't want to risk it.*

They would never want Kylie to feel like they took advantage. At least not that way. They were definitely going to take advantage of her. For the rest of their lives.

Come and join us, Radic ordered.

Tinral smiled and dried his hands. Walking over to the couch, he saw Radic had kept his hands to himself, which they both had more or less managed. Just offering an arm here, a hand brush there, nothing too overt after they had practically pounced on Kylie in Markus's foyer.

As Tinral approached, Kylie's head turned in his direction and tracked him from the waist down. He watched as she squeezed her legs together. Did she know the show she was giving them in those leggings? In her skirts, the two of them had guessed at the action, but now they could see it. Not that their jeans were doing much to hide their desire, and with her insistence to not look at their faces, she was getting an eyeful each time her eyes latched onto their zippers.

Walking right up to them, Tinral sat down to Kylie's left, sandwiching her between them. As he sat, he draped his arm over her shoulders, trailing his fingers along her exposed skin, and Radic moved his hand onto her thigh. At their actions, Kylie's pulse skyrocketed. When she did nothing more than let a small whimper escape, they both leaned toward her and feathered kisses along each side of her neck. Her sugary smell wrapped around them as she tipped her head back to grant them better access.

She tastes even better than her aura, Tinral moaned. Radic's answering noise was on just this side of feral.

"Is this okay?" Radic asked against her skin with more control than Tinral thought he had of himself.

"We won't do anything you don't want," Tinral assured her.

Her hands slid to each of their thighs and squeezed, which was encouraging, but not enough.

"You need to tell us it's okay," Radic growled beneath her ear. He was so close to snapping.

Kylie shivered and breathed out, "Yes."

Thank the devil, Radic grunted.

Practicing as much restraint as possible, they encouraged her to turn sideways on the couch. Since Tinral was still feeling calm and patient, they put her back to him.

She's closed her eyes again, Radic said unhappily.

We'll get there. Don't worry.

"Bend your knee," Tinral whispered in her ear.

Kylie leaned into him and bent her right leg, allowing Radic to pull it past him and against the back of the couch. Scooting forward, Radic positioned himself between her legs on his knees. He leaned over her, tipping her head to the left to give Tinral better access to her neck. Then, slowly, Radic lowered his head until his lips caressed Kylie's. Radic's pleasure vibrated in Tinral's head. Apparently, her lips were even more sinful than her skin. Tinral couldn't wait for a taste. He could almost feel how her lips parted for Radic when their tongues tangled.

At Kylie's needy moan and Radic's silent suggestion, Tinral slid his hands up the sides of her body and around to cup her breasts over her sweater. They fit perfectly.

You have to feel for yourself, Tinral murmured, sliding one hand back down to Kylie's hip.

Radic's hand took Tinral's place and together they squeezed. Kylie's legs fell further apart, and her hands tugged on Radic's shirt. He leaned back and obliged her, stripping his shirt off, while Tinral divested her of her pink sweater. A peek down at her revealed a lacy white confection offering her breasts to them. Together, they groaned at the sight and grew harder.

Tinral made himself a cradle for Kylie to lean back into. As she settled in against him and his hard-on, he swept his hands along her exposed arms and watched goosebumps spring up. Mesmerized, Radic followed the trail with kisses until he reached Kylie's lips again and her hands started skimming along his skin.

Now that they had her right where they wanted her, Radic's agitation lessened slightly. He couldn't get enough of Kylie's hands on his skin. A quick glance at Tinral told him it didn't just feel good. Her hands looked good against his skin, too.

I need more, Tinral said.

Instantly, Radic pulled Kylie up to her feet with him and off of Tinral. With a flick of his fingers, her bra joined their shirts. Tinral's shirt landed on the pile a second later, and he stood to ditch his jeans, too.

Good idea, Radic muttered, dropping one of his own hands from Kylie's soft skin to his zipper.

Tinral slid his hands along Kylie's sides and down to her hips, hooking his fingers into her leggings. "May I?" he asked.

Breaking her lips from Radic's, she tipped her head back and gasped, "Please." Her voice broke a little, telling them she needed them just as much as they needed her. The last week had been hell, but it was some solace to know it had been so on all sides. And now they were remedying all their suffering. Tinral didn't waste any time peeling her leggings down, though he did pause for a second to sink his teeth into a globe of her ass and to lick the indentations his teeth left behind.

Radic helped Kylie step out of her leggings as his control slipped a little further. "Look at you, Gorgeous." he growled out. Nipping her ear, he added, "Swathed in shadows. Every inch delectable. You're the best nightmare come true. We're going to ruin you tonight. How does that sound? Tongued to ruination? Hmm. That sounds like one hell of a way to go. We already know you taste delicious. I can't wait to find out if every inch of you tastes just as good."

Tinral almost laughed at how Radic was running his mouth; what Kylie must think of being called "the best nightmare come true" when she hadn't caught onto the fact they were demons would be a fun conversation for later. She might have missed that particular endearment entirely with everything else Radic was saying.

With her finally naked, they both stepped back to admire her. Each taking one of her hands, so she wasn't left adrift. Every inch of her was perfect.

"What are you doing?" Kylie asked, still breathless from their attentions.

"Just taking in the view," Radic said with appreciation. She blushed so prettily as she realized they were both just staring at her body. They guided her back to the couch and sat her down.

Tinral leaned in and took a taste of her lips. They were divine.

I know, right, Radic said. *Move down,* he added. *Let's give her a view.*

Following Radic's direction, Tinral slid down Kylie's body and sunk to his knees between her legs. Radic climbed onto the couch beside Kylie and lowered his head over her chest, blowing a stream of air over her nipples, making them tighten. Then he pulled one nipple into his mouth as Tinral dragged his tongue through her folds. Holy sulfur, did she taste good.

Her fingernails scratched along each of their scalps as she grabbed onto them and urged them to keep going. They both smiled and settled in to take her for a ride — or two.

Radic kept his touch light no matter how much Kylie arched up to offer him more. He wanted to drive her insane. Tinral was taking a different approach and pushing her higher and higher with each swirl of his tongue. They both knew that Tinral aimed to please while Radic was more than happy to tease first. Both approaches had their place and combined, it was just what Kylie needed.

Just before Kylie hurtled into her orgasm, Tinral thrust two fingers into her hard, and Radic bit the side of her breast to provide just a touch of sting. The dual actions combined with Tinral's incessant licks forced her screaming over the edge.

Chapter 10

Madame Abby

"There's the money shot!" Lucinda shouted with glee while pointing at the projection.

Purlin choked on her cocktail and sputtered as Beatrice patted her on the back, snorting so hard her eyes teared up.

"Dear, I've told you, you're not using that right," Royal said, turning an impressive shade of red for a vampire. Madame Abby had heard that it took about a hundred years for a newly turned vampire to lose the ability to blush, but it was still a strange sight to see.

Other than the fact Lucinda had indeed used the wrong term — Kylie coming on Tinral's face was not the correct usage of money shot — the watch-party was definitely a success. She had timed it just right. Thank goodness the demons had held off for a few days. It was quite impressive restraint on their part.

"I'm so happy I made it tonight," Sulnar said, leaning over to Ervin. He'd been a late arrival and the guest who would have been most likely to forgo this watch-party, in Madame Abby's estimation. Being a demon himself, he likely knew Radic and Tinral personally. Very often, her regulars skipped the watch-party when their kind was one of the participants. But Sulnar had made a point to tell her he wouldn't miss this.

Smiling contentedly at her success, Madame Abby rose and took a dramatic bow. Her guests applauded her, or maybe they applauded Kylie and her delicious performance. Either way, it was satisfying. Especially for Kylie, since neither of her demons had come up for air and both seemed intent on bringing her a second O on the tails of the first.

Taking advantage of the repeat performance, Madame Abby circulated through her guests with a pitcher of her custom glowing blue cocktail that she'd matched to the demons' eyes. As she refilled glasses, she kept her smirks to herself. As always, her guests were getting hot and bothered. But keeping it under control. A few of the gentlemen were discreetly adjusting themselves. Other guests were breathing a little faster than necessary. Still, they respected the house rules — no action while still on the premises. They could do whatever they wanted when they left, but she wasn't hosting an orgy. Just a watch-party.

The bouncers turned their rapt attention from the projection and to the door. Past them, Madame Abby could see her last two expected guests: Terry and Nat Hatmore, two witches. She hurried over to make sure they got settled before their entertainment changed positions.

Chapter 11

Kylie

"Perfect," Tinral sighed from between her legs. Radic eased his mouth off her breast with a few lingering nips and made a noise of agreement.

Kylie's head was still spinning when she felt their hair slipping out from between her fingers. She almost forgot that she couldn't look them in the face, but she shut her eyes before the worst could happen. She whimpered helplessly when Tinral withdrew his fingers from her with a slow slide.

Then, for a moment, neither of them was touching her. She felt bereft.

Thankfully, that didn't last long. They helped her stand up and turn around.

"Knees on the couch," Radic directed. She balanced there, feeling a hand on each butt cheek and on each breast. A simultaneous pluck of her nipples had her hands grasping onto the back cushion for dear life.

Somehow, the two continued to synchronize their movements and spanked her at the same time, causing her to push her breasts harder into their hands. Gently, they pulled on her nipples, urging her to move to her elbows on the back of the couch. Feeling feisty, Kylie wiggled her butt and received two more spanks, not quite as well synchronized, but more than enough to elicit a moan from her lips.

"Tease," Tinral chastised.

"I don't have to be," she joked back.

"We'll see about that," Radic said.

Both their hands slid from her breasts and down her back. Tinral's on her right disappeared completely, but Radic's spanking hand took its place with a stinging slap before grabbing onto her hips.

A thumb running over her lips made her jump.

"It's just me," Tinral said.

"And me," Radic said, as he pushed the head of his cock against her pussy. She gasped and Tinral's thumb slid into her mouth. She swirled her tongue around it and sucked when he tried to withdraw it.

"If there's anything you don't want to do, just tell us." Tinral's voice sounded strangled above her. Kylie couldn't help but grin and release his thumb.

"I definitely want," she said, licking her lips and trying to push back against Radic. "I've been thinking about this all week."

Behind her, Radic muttered something that sounded a lot like, "Burning flames," but Kylie wasn't sure.

"Open," Tinral said as he stroked her cheek. She dropped her jaw and was rewarded with his cock sliding against her tongue. He tasted so good, almost like a rich candy she couldn't identify but would dream about for years to come. His moan was music to her ears.

Safe with the knowledge that neither of their faces were within view, Kylie opened her eyes so she could watch Tinral pump his hips into her mouth. It was a marvelous view. But once Radic started to rub his cock up and down her slit, teasing her clit before almost sliding into her, she had to close her eyes again. It was almost too much pleasure.

After what seemed like an eternity of torture, Radic gave a hard thrust and buried his cock in her while her mouth was full of Tinral. She moaned around him, her whole body shaking. They both cursed.

Tinral's hands bunched her hair behind her head, holding it perfectly still while he withdrew. Radic's cock slowly retreated too, leaving her wanting. He also steadied her. Panting, she waited. Her anticipation and frustration built, and she was on the verge of begging when Tinral gave her the tip of his cock again. But no more. She swirled her tongue around it. Trying to tell him she was all in.

That was when Radic started up again.

He struck a steady rhythm in no time that had her thankful that Tinral was holding himself steady. With each of Radic's thrusts, her mouth filled a little more with Tinral's cock. Kylie's whole body felt ready to give out, but the two men held her up. Their grunts and moans filled the room, and Kylie gave herself over to sensation, feeling her pleasure build and build.

When Radic leaned over her and reached around for her clit, he whispered in her ear: "You look so good sucking on Tinral's cock while you take mine. I can't wait to see how your mouth feels while he's fucking you."

That was all she needed to fall over the edge into her third orgasm.

Both Radic and Tinral followed her off the cliff. Radic pumped through his, making her eyes roll back with each thrust, and she did her best to lap up every last drop that Tinral gave her before he let his dick fall from her lips.

None of them moved for a moment while they caught their breath. Kylie wasn't sure she could move, but she suspected that they'd take care of that for her. They were very adept at putting her where they wanted her. And she really liked where they wanted her.

"Stay still," Radic said. Tinral's hands left her hair, so she guessed Radic was talking to her and not to Tinral. A moment later, a warm cloth made her jerk as it slid between her legs, cleaning her up.

"Sit down to the left," Tinral suggested after they finished. She did just that, and they eased her down and back into a seated position.

Then, they each straddled one of her legs, spreading her back open and causing tingles to shoot through her. Her hands instantly went to each of their hips. She watched as Tinral and Radic threaded their fingers together in front of her. A big fan of those hands, she whimpered at the memory of what the two had just done to her. And the more that Radic promised.

Out of the corner of her eyes, she saw their outer arms move toward her. A hand threaded into her hair on each side of her head and tipped her face up to theirs. She instantly closed her eyes.

"Trust us, Kylie," Tinral coaxed.

"Open your eyes," Radic ordered gently.

Not wanting to hurt either of them, but desperate to believe that they'd be okay, Kylie blinked her eyes open.

Glowing blue eyes stared back at her — as in, their entire eyes were glowing blue. They had no whites, irises, or pupils, but she had no doubt they were both looking right at her. Her heart felt too big for her chest. Her hands clenched on their hips and they both smiled down at her. They were perfect. So good-looking it should have been a crime. Radic's nose looked like it had been broken once, but it just made him look more rugged; Kylie imagined the effect he'd have dressed in his suit and knew he would be doubly devastating. Tinral had a strong brow that gave him a brooding demeanor that would make any woman want to stroke and pet him to contentment.

Kylie's mind flashed back to a book her adoptive mom had shown her. There was a character with glowing blue eyes in it. A demon, if she recalled correctly.

"Oh, my," she breathed out, unable to peel her eyes off them. "Does this mean I'm a sinner?"

"Even better," Radic said with a grin.

"You're our demoness," Tinral finished.

"Demoness?" she repeated.

The pair stood up and playfully dragged her after them. Her legs felt like Jello, but since she was pretty sure they were heading to a bedroom, she mustered the energy to follow. Kylie's breath caught when she saw the bed. It was massive. Like a bed and a half.

"The middle is yours, of course," Tinral said. Kylie loved the smile in his voice and had to giggle at how much fun it was to be sandwiched between them.

To her chagrin, they didn't take her straight to the bed to begin again. Instead, they spun around so that they were all facing a floor-to-ceiling mirror. Greedily, Kylie's eyes ate up their naked bodies on the way up to their faces. They were both gorgeous.

"Look at your eyes, love," Radic murmured, unperturbed by her perusal.

Forcing herself to stop looking at them, Kylie looked at herself. Her heart stuttered in her chest. She took a half-step forward, catching herself with a hand against the cold mirror, and her body broke out in goosebumps.

Her irises. They were glowing blue like Tinral and Radic's eyes.

"When you first lay eyes on your soulmates' faces," Tinral said with care for the s's.

"Death you will see," Radic said to finish Madame Abby's fortune.

Kylie's eyes widened further, and she flitted her gaze from one demon to the other. The overwhelming happiness she'd felt the moment she looked upon them meant that they were hers. And she was theirs. This was where she fit in.

And apparently, she was a demoness.

Chapter 12

Madame Abby

With a wave of her hand, Madame Abby cut the projection from her crystal ball on a shot of the two demons standing behind Kylie at the mirror, all their eyes aglow. The juxtaposition of two born demons and a turned demon's eyes was a perfect ending. Still, her audience groaned.

"They might go for another round," Ervin protested, waving at the screen.

"Perhaps, but we'll call it a night," Madame Abby said.

"They'll definitely do at least one more round tonight," Sulnar assured Ervin with a knowing smirk. Madame Abby didn't doubt his estimation. The three of them were nowhere near sated. But she did like to give her matches some level of privacy.

"As always, it's been a pleasure," Lucinda called over her shoulder, dragging Royal out the door with her for their own night of fun. The first time that had happened, Royal had been embarrassed, but he'd gotten over it by the third occurrence. Madame Abby assumed he had rather spectacular evenings after each of her showings. Lucinda was rumored to have always been remarkably enthusiastic before settling down with Royal. That likely hadn't changed. Their departure let in a burst of cool night air that seemed to signal the official end of the evening.

Another few guests left quickly, particularly those who came with someone. Ervin left with Purlin and Burty, likely to enact their own version of a threesome; knowing the two ladies like she did, Madame Abby suspected Ervin would shortly be playing the base of a double cowgirl. The last to leave was a group of singles who lingered to finish their drinks before heading out. It sounded like they'd be going to a club down the street with Sulnar leading the way with hopes of finding bedmates who hadn't enjoyed the watch-party.

With the last guests gone, Madame Abby sent the bouncers off with a nice tip and wondered if they would hit the club too, go home to partners, or maybe even go home with each other. She liked not knowing. It let her imagine any scenario that tickled her fancy. They were *fine*-looking men. But then again, Stone Defense only seemed to employ guards who looked like they could go all night and leave their partner gasping for more.

The only downside to nailing this prediction was that Madame Abby knew she'd be getting an angry visit from Ms. Skye, Kylie's adoptive mom. That this was Kylie's destiny wouldn't matter to the angel. She'd just be upset her daughter had turned demon. But the fall had been so sweet to watch.

On that note, Madame Abby locked up her shop and headed home. Her bangle skirt filled the night with music as she hurried along. She was looking forward to a little alone time of her own to relive the best moments of the watch-party.

Epilogue

Radic & Tinral

Three months later

TINRAL ADJUSTED HIS TIE and stared at the window display of Mystical Moments, Madame Abby's shop on X street. Between him and Radic, Kylie stood with a hand hooked in the crook of each of their elbows.

Is this a good idea? Radic asked, again.

Probably not, but she wants it, Tinral answered. She had insisted once she'd found out that Madame Abby hadn't sent her to Markus's house on a whim and was actually rumored to dabble in matchmaking along with reading fortunes.

"You're doing it again, aren't you?" Kylie accused the two of them.

"Sorry," Radic murmured.

Kylie just shook her head at them and started pulling them toward the door. Radic and Tinral hadn't realized that Kylie wouldn't get the ability to silently communicate with them, and she didn't like to be left out. Well, unless they were planning something special to do to her. She seemed to particularly appreciate how well they synchronized in the bedroom and didn't care in the least that they were discussing her in those moments. But the rest of the time, she didn't like to be excluded unnecessarily. Speaking aloud between the two of them didn't feel natural, but for Kylie, they were making an effort.

Tinral reached out and held the door open, letting Radic escort Kylie inside. Neither he nor Radic had been to a mystic shop that catered to both occult and human customers. It was surprising that Madame Abby had chosen to straddle the divide between the paranormal and otherwise. Most fates of her talent charged a premium and lived deeply ensconced in paranormal communities.

Like many of the less discreet paranormal, Radic and Tinral preferred visiting paranormal-only establishments because they caused no panic there. It had hurt them when Kylie encountered it for the first time. She hadn't anticipated that her glowing irises would unsettle normal humans, especially those who didn't realize there was a paranormal neighborhood nearby (or, more to the point, in existence at all). In comparison, meeting her mother, Ms. Skye, and seeing her devastation at losing her daughter to demons had been child's play. Kylie's mother had rallied after her initial shock and showed the grandeur of her angelic heart by continuing to accept Kylie as her own, even if she could never hug her daughter again without burning her alive. But seeing how hurt Kylie was by strangers she didn't even know, that had been unbearable.

Madame Abby's shop was set up differently than Tinral and Radic had seen in other shops. The most obvious difference was that the wares were labeled with extensive descriptions. Each witch's potion had its typical name, but then there were a lot of details about what it did and what "moment" it would produce. The crystals and incense had similar descriptive cards to guide the uninitiated. Oddly, the place was covered with draped sequin curtains in red that Radic and Tinral found rather distasteful outside of a vampire's boudoir. But maybe that was what humans expected in a place like this.

A woman in her thirties hustled out from the back as Tinral pulled the door closed behind the three of them. She jangled as she moved, and when she cleared the shelves that separated them, it was easy to see why. She wore a bangle skirt tied around her hips and the dangling coins bounced with each sway of her hips.

"Madame Abby," Kylie greeted warmly.

"Kylie," she answered with a grin at all three of them. "I expected you last month."

She did? Radic asked.

That is when Kylie started talking about coming here, Tinral answered. That was also when Markus returned home early from his trip to see his family, and he was very much not alone.

"I suspect you know who these two are," Kylie said, giving their arms a squeeze.

"I do," Madame Abby said. "It's wonderful to see that everything is working out."

"We just wanted to come by and thank you for helping us get together."

"We?"

Kylie sighed as if put upon, which made Radic grin and Tinral wink at Madame Abby. They were putty in Kylie's hands and would do just about anything she wanted, including thanking a matchmaker they never hired or met before.

“I wanted to, and they are humoring me I suspect,” Kylie groused with a playful glare at each of them.

“They surely understand that matchmaking is a pastime and not something for which I expect recognition. I don’t exactly advertise the service,” Madame Abby explained.

But she sure does like it, Tinral muttered. There was an extra gleam in her eyes that lit up when talking about matchmaking.

At least she’s not gloating or making jokes, Radic concurred. They’d been worried about a quip or two about threesomes. Many people were uncomfortable with anything that diverged from the widely accepted single pairing. Though, paranormals were more open-minded than most in Radic’s and Tinral’s experience.

“But since you’re here,” Madame Abby continued, oblivious to their exchange, “have a look around.”

It turned out to be a blessing in disguise that Mystical Moments had such extensive descriptions for its wares. Tinral and Radic hadn’t considered that every item would be new to Kylie. She was fascinated to learn that a Flex Potion could help a gargoyle skip a stone cycle. That strategically placing crystals throughout the house could create energy fields to boost motivation or mood was something she’d never considered. They didn’t fight in the least when Kylie picked up a set of purple haze incense sticks and insisted they get them. The scent combination was purported to enhance tantric states and sensitivity to touch.

When they brought the purchase up to Madame Abby, she waved away their payment saying that it was on the house and gave them a number of helpful tips about how to get the scent to circle around them to increase its efficacy.

We might have to come back here, Radic said as they left.

I had no idea that was what purple haze did, Tinral admitted. He was in total agreement.

"Her shop is so much fun! I didn't look around at all last time. We did my reading, and then I hurried off trying not to look at anyone," Kylie shared. "But now, you'll have to tell me what you two talked about because I know you weren't just standing there being silent the whole time."

They both grinned at their demoness. She was always going to keep them on their toes, which was just fine by them.

If you want to read about more of the Mystical Matchmaker series, the next book is *Vampire Lube*: https://daysgrant.com/vampirelube/

If you're looking for a longer read, make sure to check out my series The Mavens, which starts with *Touchy Talents: https://daysgrant.com/touchytalents/*

If you want to stay up-to-date with all the latest writing news and my upcoming releases, sign up for my newsletter: https://www.daysgrant.com/contact-2/

About the author

Day S. Grant's fascination with *the other* has grown throughout her life. She believes that things aren't as different as they seem. Her books consistently introduce opposites, others, and new perspectives that shift how people see the world. You can see this throughout her books in both her Mystical Matchmaker series and The Mavens.

A traveler at heart, when Day S. isn't traveling through the pages of a book with a steaming cup of tea, she is exploring new places. She loves nature and likes finding interesting trees to photograph. When she can, she takes her cats with her on her adventures.

Her passion for creating isn't contained to the blank page, but also manifests in doodles and in a life-long sewing hobby. She enjoys making clothes for herself and, on occasion, for her very patient cats.

Learn more about Day S. Grant and her upcoming releases by going to her website and signing up for her newsletter: Day S. Grant Gossips.

Also by Day S. Grant

The Mavens

Touchy Talents

Shell Shocked (coming 2026)

In the Mavens' world

Opposites Collide

Opposites Clash (coming 2026)

Mystical Matchmaker

A Demon Sandwich

Vampire Lube (coming 2026)

Made in the USA
Coppell, TX
17 March 2026

73642282R00049